Thomas the Tank Engine & Friends

A BRITT ALLCROFT COMPANY PRODUCTION

Based on The Railway Series by The Rev W Awdry
© Gullane (Thomas) LLC 2002

Visit the Thomas & Friends web site at www.thomasthetankengine.com

ISBN 0-439-33841-7

12 11 10 9 8 7 6 5 4 3 2 1   2 3 4 5 6 7/0
Printed in the U.S.A.
First Scholastic printing, January 2002

Paint Pots and the Royal Queen

by
The REV. W. AWDRY

SCHOLASTIC INC.

New York   Toronto   London   Auckland   Sydney
Mexico City   New Delhi   Hong Kong   Buenos Aires

The stations on the line were being painted. The engines were surprised.

"The Queen is coming," said the painters. The engines in their shed were excited and wondered who would pull the Royal Train.

"I'm too old to pull important trains," said Edward sadly.

"I'm in disgrace," Gordon said gloomily. "Sir Topham Hatt would never choose me."

"He'll choose me, of course," boasted James the Red Engine.

"You!" Henry snorted, "*You* can't climb hills. He will ask *me* to pull it, *and* I'll have a new coat of paint. You wait and see."

The days passed. Henry puffed about proudly, quite sure that he would be the Royal Engine.

One day when it rained, his Driver and Fireman stretched a tarpaulin from the cab to the tender, to keep themselves dry.

Henry puffed into the big station. A painter was climbing a ladder above the line. Henry's smoke puffed upward; it was thick and black. The painter choked and couldn't see. He missed his footing on the ladder, dropped his paint pot, and fell plop onto Henry's tarpaulin.

The paint poured over Henry's boiler and trickled down each side. The paint pot perched on his dome.

The painter clambered down and shook his brush at Henry.

"You spoil my clean paint with your dirty smoke," he said, "and then you take the whole lot, and make me go and fetch some more." He stumped away crossly.

Sir Topham Hatt pushed through the crowd.

"You look like an iced cake, Henry," he said. "*That* won't do for the Royal Train. I must make other arrangements."

He walked over to the yard.

Gordon and Thomas saw him coming, and both began to speak.

"Please Sir . . . "

"One at a time," smiled Sir Topham Hatt. "Yes Gordon?"

"May Thomas have his branch line again?"

"Hm," said Sir Topham Hatt, "well Thomas?"

"Please, Sir, can Gordon pull coaches now?"

Sir Topham Hatt pondered.

"Hm . . . you've both been quite good lately, and you deserve a treat . . . When the Queen comes, Edward will go in front and clear the line, Thomas will look after the coaches, and Gordon . . . will pull the train."

"Ooooh Sir!" said the engines happily.

The great day came. Percy, Toby, Henry, and James worked hard bringing people to town.

Thomas sorted all their coaches in the yard.

"*Peep! Peep! Peep!* They're coming!" Edward steamed in, looking smart with flags and bright paint.

Two minutes passed—five—seven—ten. "*Poop, Poop!*" Everyone knew that whistle, and a mighty cheer went up as the Queen's train glided into the station.

Gordon was spotless, and his brass shone. Like Edward, he was decorated with flags, but on his buffer he proudly carried the Royal Arms.

The Queen was met by Sir Topham Hatt, and before doing anything else, she thanked him for their splendid run.

"Not at all, Your Majesty," he said, "thank *you*."

"We have read," said the Queen to Sir Topham Hatt, "a great deal about your engines. May we see them please?"

So he led the way to where all the engines were waiting.

"*Peep! Peep!*" whistled Toby and Percy, "they're coming!"

"*Sh-sh! Sh-sh!*" hissed Henry and James.

But Toby and Percy were too excited to care.

Sir Topham Hatt told the Queen their names, and she talked to each engine. Then she turned to go.

Percy bubbled over "Three cheers for the Queen!" he called.

"*Peeep! Peeep! Peeep!*" whistled all the engines.

Sir Topham Hatt held his ears, but the Queen, smiling, waved to the engines till she passed the gate.

The next day, the Queen spoke specially to Thomas, who fetched her coaches, and to Edward and Gordon who took her away; and no engines ever felt prouder than Thomas, and Edward, and Gordon the Big Engine.

Now flip the book over to start another Thomas & Friends adventure.